Thomas'

Photographs by David Mitton, Kenny McArthur, and Terry Permane

Random House New York

Thomas the Tank Engine & Friends®

A BRITT ALLCROFT COMPANY PRODUCTION

Based on The Railway Series by The Reverend W Awdry

www.randomhouse.com/kids/thomas www.thomasandfriends.com

Library of Congress Control Number: 2006922097

ISBN-13: 978-0-375-84013-5 ISBN-10: 0-375-84013-3
PRINTED IN CHINA 10 9 8 7 6 5 4 3 2 1 First Edition

Contents

Thomas
Gets Tricked
and Other Stories
Based on The Railway Series
by the Rev. W. Awdry
As seen on the television show
Shining Time Station

Trouble
for
Thomas
and Other Stories
Based on The Railway Series
by the Rev. W. Awdry
As seen on the television show
Shining Time Station

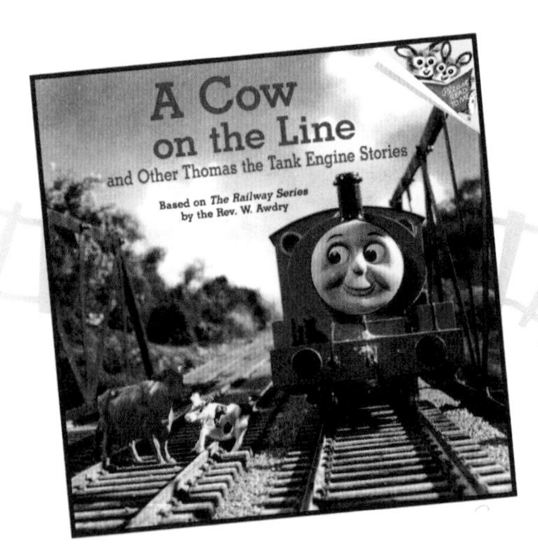
A Cow
on the Line
and Other Thomas the Tank Engine Stories
Based on The Railway Series
by the Rev. W. Awdry

JAMES IN A MESS
and Other Thomas the Tank Engine Stories
Based on The Railway Series by the Rev. W. Awdry

Diesel's Devious Deed
and Other Thomas the Tank Engine Stories
Based on The Railway Series by the Rev. W. Awdry

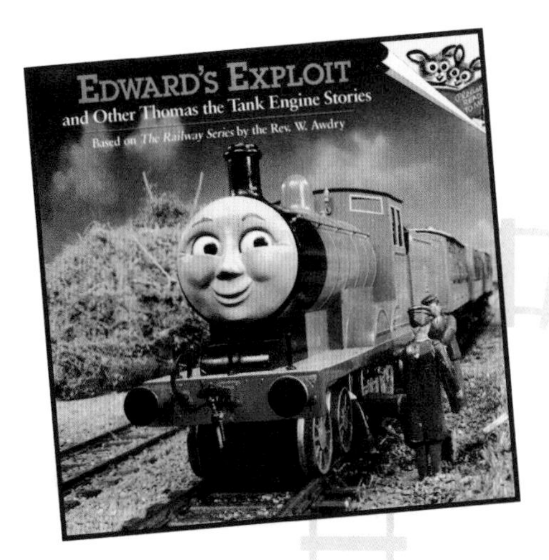
EDWARD'S EXPLOIT
and Other Thomas the Tank Engine Stories
Based on The Railway Series by the Rev. W. Awdry

Thomas Gets Tricked

Thomas is a tank engine who lives at a big station on the Island of Sodor.

He's a cheeky little engine with six small wheels, a short stumpy funnel, a short stumpy boiler, and a short stumpy dome.

He's a fussy little engine, too, always pulling coaches about, ready for the big engines to take on long journeys. And when trains come in, he pulls the empty coaches away so that the big engines can go and rest.

Thomas thinks no engine works as hard as he does. He loves playing tricks on them, including Gordon, the biggest and proudest engine of all. Thomas likes to tease Gordon with his whistle.

"Wake up, lazybones. Why don't you work hard like me?"

One day after pulling the big Express, Gordon had arrived back at the sidings very tired. He was just going to sleep when Thomas came up in his teasing way.

"Wake up, lazybones. Do some hard work for a change. You can't catch me!" And off Thomas ran, laughing.

Instead of going to sleep again, Gordon thought how he could get back at Thomas.

One morning, Thomas wouldn't wake up. His Driver and Fireman couldn't make him start. His fire went out and there was not enough steam. It was nearly time for the Express. People were waiting, but the coaches weren't ready.

At last, Thomas started. "Oh, dear! Oh, dear!" he yawned. He fussed into the station, where Gordon was waiting.

"Hurry up, you," said Gordon.

"Hurry yourself," replied Thomas.

Gordon, the proud engine, began making his plan to teach Thomas a lesson for teasing him. Almost before the coaches had stopped moving, Gordon reversed quickly and was coupled to the train.

"Get in quickly, please," he whistled.

Thomas usually pushed behind the big trains to help them start. But he was always uncoupled first.

This time, Gordon started so quickly they forgot to uncouple Thomas. Gordon's chance had come!

"Come on, come on," puffed Gordon to the coaches.

The train went faster and faster—too fast for Thomas. He wanted to stop, but he couldn't! "*Peep! Peep!* Stop! Stop!"

"Hurry, hurry, hurry," laughed Gordon.

"You can't get away. You can't get away," laughed the coaches.

Poor Thomas was going faster than he had ever gone before. He was out of breath and his wheels hurt him, but he had to go on.

"I shall never be the same again," he thought sadly. "My wheels will be quite worn out."

At last, they stopped at a station. Thomas was uncoupled, and he felt very silly and exhausted.

Next he went onto a turntable, thinking of everyone laughing at him, and then he ran onto a siding out of the way.

"Well, little Thomas," chuckled Gordon. "Now you know what hard work means, don't you?"

Poor Thomas couldn't answer. He had no breath. He just puffed slowly away to rest and had a long, long drink.

"Maybe I don't have to tease Gordon to feel important," Thomas thought to himself. And he puffed slowly home.

Come Out, Henry!

Once, an engine attached to a train was afraid of a few drops of rain. It went into a tunnel and squeaked through its funnel and wouldn't come out again.

The engine's name is Henry. His Driver and Fireman argued with him, but he would not move.

"The rain will spoil my lovely green paint and red stripes," he said.

The Conductor blew his whistle till he had no more breath and waved his flag till his arms ached. But Henry still stayed in the tunnel and blew steam at him.

"I'm not going to spoil my lovely green paint and red stripes for you."

Then—along came Sir Topham Hatt, the man in charge of all the engines on the Island of Sodor.

"We will pull you out," said Sir Topham Hatt. But Henry only blew steam at him.

Everyone pulled except Sir Topham Hatt. "Because," he said, "my doctor has forbidden me to pull." But still Henry stayed in the tunnel.

Then they tried pushing from the other end. Sir Topham Hatt said, "One, two, three, push!" But he didn't help. "My doctor has forbidden me to push," he said.

They pushed and pushed and pushed. But still Henry stayed in the tunnel.

At last, Thomas came along. The Conductor waved his red flag and stopped him.

Everyone argued with Henry. "Look, it has stopped raining," they said.

"Yes, but it will begin again soon," said Henry. "And what would become of my green paint with red stripes then?"

Thomas pushed and puffed, and pushed as hard as ever he could.

But still Henry stayed in the tunnel.

Eventually, even Sir Topham Hatt gave up.

"We shall take away your rails," he said, "and leave you here until you're ready to come out of the tunnel."

They took up the old rails and built a wall in front of Henry so that other engines wouldn't bump into him. All Henry could do was to watch the trains rushing through the other tunnel. He was very sad because he thought no one would ever see his lovely green paint with red stripes again.

As time went on, Edward and Gordon would often pass by.

Edward would say, "*Peep, peep!* Hello."

And Gordon would say, "*Poop, poop, poop.* Serves you right."

Poor Henry had no steam to answer. His fire had gone out. Soot and dirt from the tunnel had spoiled his lovely green paint and red stripes, anyway.

How long do you think Henry will stay in the tunnel before he overcomes his fear of the rain and then decides to journey out again?

Henry to the Rescue

Gordon always pulled the big Express. He was proud of being the only engine strong enough to do so. It was full of important people like Sir Topham Hatt, and Gordon was seeing how fast he could go.

"Hurry, hurry, hurry," he said.

"Trickety-trock, trickety-trock, trickety-trock," said the coaches.

In a minute, Gordon would see the tunnel where Henry stood, bricked up and lonely.

"Oh, dear," thought Henry. "Why did I worry about rain spoiling my lovely coat of paint? I'd like to come out of the tunnel." But Henry didn't know how to ask.

"I'm going to *'poop, poop'* at Henry," said Gordon.

He was almost there when—*Wheeeeeeeeshshsh*—and there was proud Gordon going slower and slower in a cloud of steam.

His Driver stopped the train.

"What has happened to me?" asked Gordon. "I feel so weak."

"You've burst your safety valve," said the Driver. "You can't pull the train anymore."

"Oh, dear," said Gordon. "We were going so nicely, too. And look—there's Henry—laughing at me."

Everyone came to see Gordon.

"Humph," said Sir Topham Hatt. "These big engines are always causing me trouble. Send for another engine at once."

While the Conductor went to find one, they uncoupled Gordon, who had enough puff to slink onto the siding out of the way.

Edward was the only engine left. "I'll come and try," he said.

"Pooh!" said Gordon. "That's no use. Edward can't push the train."

Kind Edward puffed and pushed and pushed and puffed, but he couldn't move the heavy coaches.

"I told you so," said Gordon. "Why not let Henry try?"

"Yes," said Sir Topham Hatt, "I will. Will you help pull this train, Henry?" he asked.

"Oh, yes," said Henry.

When Henry had got up steam, he puffed out. He was dirty and covered with cobwebs. "Ooh! I'm stiff, I'm stiff," he groaned.

"Have a run to ease your joints, and find a turntable," said Sir Topham Hatt.

When Henry came back, he felt much better. Then they coupled him up.

"Peep, peep," said Edward. "I'm ready."
"Peep, peep, peep," said Henry. "So am I."
"Pull hard. We'll do it. Pull hard. We'll do it," they puffed together.

"We've done it together. We've done it together," said Edward and Henry.

"You've done it, hurray! You've done it, hurray!" sang the coaches.

Everyone was excited. Sir Topham Hatt leaned out of the window to wave at Edward and Henry, but the train was going so fast that his hat blew off into a field, where a goat ate it for tea.

They never stopped till they came to the station at the end of the line.

The passengers all said "Thank you," and Sir Topham Hatt promised Henry a new coat of paint.

On their way home, Edward and Henry helped Gordon back to the Shed.

All three engines are now great friends.

Henry doesn't mind the rain now. He knows that the best way to keep his paint nice is not to run into tunnels but to ask his Driver to rub him down when the day's work is over.

A Big Day for Thomas

Thomas the Tank Engine was grumbling to the other engines. "I spend my time pulling coaches about, ready for you to take out on journeys."

The other engines laughed.

"Why can't I pull passenger trains, too?"

"You're too impatient," they said. "You'd be sure to leave something behind."

"Rubbish," said Thomas. "I'll show you."

One night, he and Henry were alone. Henry was ill. The men worked hard, but he didn't get better.

He felt just as bad next morning.

Henry usually pulled the first train, and Thomas had to get his coaches ready.

"If Henry is ill," he thought, "perhaps I shall pull his train."

Thomas ran to find the coaches. “Come along, come along,” he fussed.

“There’s plenty of time. There’s plenty of time,” they grumbled.

Thomas took them to the platform and wanted to run round in front at once.

But his Driver wouldn’t let him. “Don’t be impatient, Thomas.”

Thomas waited and waited.

The people got in. The Conductor and Station Master walked up and down. The Porter banged the doors, and still Henry didn’t come.

Thomas got more and more excited.

Sir Topham Hatt came to see what was the matter, and the Conductor and the Station Master told him about Henry.

"Find another engine," he ordered.

"There's only Thomas," they said.

"You'll have to do it, then, Thomas. Be quick now!"

So Thomas ran round to the front and backed down on the coaches, ready to start.

"Let's not be impatient," said his Driver. "We'll wait till everything is ready."

But Thomas was too excited to listen.

What happened then no one knows. Perhaps they forgot to couple Thomas to the train. Or perhaps the Driver pulled the lever by mistake.

Anyhow, Thomas started without his coaches.

As he passed the first signal tower, men waved and shouted. But he didn't stop.

"They're waving because I'm such a splendid engine," he thought importantly. "Henry says it's hard to pull trains, but I think it's easy."

"Hurry, hurry, hurry," he puffed, pretending to be like Gordon.

"People have never seen me pulling a train before. It's nice of them to wave." And he whistled, "*Peep, peep!* Thank you."

Then he came to a signal at "DANGER."

"Bother," he thought. "I must stop, and I was going so nicely, too. What a nuisance signals are." He blew an angry *"Peep, peep"* on his whistle.

The Signalman ran up. “Hullo, Thomas,” he said. “What are you doing here?”

“I’m pulling a train,” said Thomas. “Can’t you see?”

“Where are your coaches, then?”

Thomas looked back. “Why, bless me,” he said, “if we haven’t left them behind.”

“Yes,” said the Signalman. “You’d better go back quickly and fetch them.”

Poor Thomas was so sad he nearly cried.

“Cheer up,” said his Driver. “Let’s go back quickly and try again.”

At the station, all the passengers were talking at once. They were telling Sir Topham Hatt what a bad railway it was.

But when Thomas came back, they saw how sad he was and couldn’t be cross.

He was coupled to the train, and this time he really pulled it.

Afterwards, the other engines laughed at Thomas and said, “Look, there’s Thomas, who wanted to pull a train but forgot about the coaches.” But Thomas had already learned not to make the same mistake again.

Trouble for Thomas

Thomas the Tank Engine wouldn't stop being a nuisance. Night after night, he kept the other engines awake.

"I'm tired of pushing coaches. I want to see the world."

The other engines didn't take much notice, for Thomas was a little engine with a long tongue.

But one night, Edward came to the Shed. He was a kind little engine and felt sorry for Thomas.

"I've got some freight cars to take home tomorrow. If you take them instead of me, I'll push coaches in the Yard."

"Thank you," said Thomas. "That will be nice."

Next morning, Edward and Thomas asked their Drivers, and when they said "Yes," Thomas ran off happily to find freight cars.

Now, the freight cars are silly and noisy. They talk a lot and don't attend to what they are doing. And, I'm sorry to say, they play tricks on an engine who is not used to them.

Edward knew all about freight cars. He warned Thomas to be careful, but Thomas was too excited to listen.

The Shunter fastened the coupling, and when the signal dropped, Thomas was ready. The Conductor blew his whistle.

"Peep! Peep!" answered Thomas, and started off.

But the freight cars weren't ready. "Oh, oh, oh!" they screamed. "Wait, Thomas, wait!"

But Thomas wouldn't wait. "Come on, come on," he puffed.

"All right, all right, don't fuss, all right, don't fuss," grumbled the cars.

Thomas began going faster and faster. *"Wheeeeeee!"* he whistled as he rushed through Henry's Tunnel.

Then he was out into the open countryside once more. They rumbled past fields and they clattered through stations.

"Hurry, hurry!" called Thomas. He was feeling very proud of himself. But the cars grew crosser and crosser.

At last, Thomas slowed down as he came to Gordon's Hill.

"Steady now, steady," warned the Driver as they reached the top. He began to put on the brakes.

"We're stopping, we're stopping," called Thomas.

"No, no, no!" answered the cars, bumping into each other. "Go on, go on."

Before the Driver could stop them, they had pushed Thomas down the hill and were rattling and laughing behind him.

Poor Thomas tried hard to stop them from making him go too fast.

"Stop pushing, stop pushing," he hissed, but the cars took no notice.

"Go on, go on," they giggled in their silly way.

Thomas was traveling much too fast, and at any moment he would reach the next station.

"There's the station. Oh, dear, what shall I do?" he cried.

They rattled straight through and swerved into the Goods Yard. Thomas shut his eyes. "I must stop!"

When he opened his eyes, he saw he had stopped just in front of the buffers. There watching him was Sir Topham Hatt.

"What are you doing here, Thomas?" he asked.

"I've brought Edward's freight cars," Thomas answered.

"Why did you come so fast?"

"I didn't mean to. I was pushed," said Thomas.

"You've got a lot to learn about freight cars, Thomas. After pushing them about here for a few weeks, you'll know almost as much about them as Edward. Then you'll be a Really Useful Engine."

Thomas Saves the Day

Every day, Sir Topham Hatt came to the station to catch his train.

"Hullo," he always said to Thomas. "Don't let the silly freight cars tease you. Remember, you have an important job as a special helper in the Train Yard."

There were lots of freight cars, and Thomas worked very hard pushing and pulling them into place.

There was also a small coach and two strange things his Driver called cranes.

"That's the breakdown train," he told Thomas. "The cranes are for lifting heavy things like engines and coaches and freight cars."

One day, Thomas was in the Yard. Suddenly he heard an engine whistling.

"Help! Help!" A freight train came rushing through much too fast. The engine was James—and he was frightened. His brake blocks were on fire!

"They're pushing me. They're pushing me," he panted.

"On, on," laughed the freight cars.

Still whistling "Help, help!" poor James disappeared.

"I'd like to teach those freight cars a lesson," said Thomas the Tank Engine.

Soon came the alarm. "James is off the line—the breakdown train—quickly!"

Thomas was coupled on, and off they went.

Thomas worked his hardest. "Hurry, hurry, hurry," he puffed. He wasn't pretending to be like Gordon. He really meant it. "Bother those freight cars and their tricks. I hope poor James isn't hurt."

James' Driver and Fireman were feeling him all over to see if he was hurt.

"Never mind, James," they said. "It was those silly freight cars and your old wooden brakes that caused the accident."

Thomas pushed the breakdown train alongside. Then he pulled away the unhurt freight cars.

"Oh, dear. Oh, dear," they groaned.

"Serves you right. Serves you right," puffed Thomas.

He was hard at work puffing backwards and forwards all afternoon. "This'll teach you a lesson. This'll teach you a lesson," he told the freight cars.

And they answered, "Yes—it—will, yes—it—will."

They left the broken cars. Then, with two cranes, they put James back on the rails. He tried to move, but he couldn't. So Thomas helped him back to the Shed.

Sir Topham Hatt was waiting anxiously for them.

"Well, Thomas," he said. "I've heard all about it, and I'm very pleased with you. You're a Really Useful Engine. James shall have some proper brakes and a new coat of paint, and you shall have a Branch Line all to yourself."

"Oh, thank you, Sir!" said Thomas.

Now Thomas is as happy as can be. He has a Branch Line and two coaches called Annie and Clarabel. He puffs proudly backwards and forwards with them all day.

He is never lonely. Edward and Henry stop quite often and tell him the news.

Gordon is always in a hurry but never forgets to say, *"Poop, poop,"* and Thomas always whistles, *"Peep, peep"* in return.

Thomas Goes Fishing

When Thomas puffed along his Branch Line, he always looked forward to something special . . . the sight of the river.

As he rumbled over the bridge, he would see people fishing. Thomas often wanted to stay and watch, but his Driver said, "No. What would Sir Topham Hatt say if we were late?" But Thomas still thought it would be lovely to stop by the river.

Every time he met another engine, he would say, "I want to fish." But they all had the same answer, "Engines don't go fishing."

"Silly stick-in-the-muds," thought Thomas.

One day, he stopped as usual to take in water at the station by the river.

"Out of order! Bother," said Thomas. "I'm thirsty."

"Never mind," said his Driver. "We'll get some water from the river."

They found a bucket and some rope and went to the bridge.

Then the Driver let the bucket down to the water. The bucket was old and had five holes. So they had to fill it, pull it up, and empty it into Thomas' tank as quickly as they could several times over.

They finished at last.

"That's good. That's good," puffed Thomas, and Annie and Clarabel ran happily behind.

Suddenly Thomas began to feel a pain in his boiler. Steam began to hiss from his safety valve in an alarming way.

"There's too much steam," said his Driver.

"Oh, dear," groaned Thomas. "I'm going to burst. I'm going to burst."

They damped down his fire and struggled on.

"I've got such a pain. I've got such a pain," Thomas hissed.

They stopped just outside the last station, uncoupled Annie and Clarabel, and ran Thomas, who was still hissing fit to burst, on a siding right out of the way.

Then, while the Conductor telephoned for an Engine Inspector, the Driver found notices in large letters, which he hung on Thomas in front and behind:

DANGER. KEEP AWAY.

Soon the Inspector and Sir Topham Hatt arrived. "Cheer up, Thomas," they said. "We'll soon put you right."

The Driver told them what had happened.

"So the feed pipe is blocked," said the Inspector. "I'll just look in the tanks."

He climbed up and peered in. Then he came down. "Excuse me, Sir. Please look in the tank and tell me what you see."

"Certainly, Inspector," replied Sir Topham Hatt.

He clambered up, looked in, and nearly fell off in surprise.

"Inspector," he whispered, "can you see fish?

"Gracious goodness me. How did the fish get there, Driver?"

"We must have fished them from the river with our bucket," replied Thomas' Driver.

"Well, Thomas. So you and your Driver have been fishing. But fish don't suit you. We must get them out."

They all took turns at fishing in Thomas' tank while Sir Topham Hatt looked on and told them how to do it.

When they had caught all the fish, they had a lovely picnic supper of fish and chips.

"That was good," said Sir Topham Hatt. "But fish don't suit you, Thomas. So you mustn't do it again."

"No, Sir, I won't," said Thomas sadly. "Engines don't go fishing. It's too uncomfortable."

Terence the Tractor

Autumn had come to the Island of Sodor.

The fields were changing from yellow stubble to brown earth.

And a tractor was hard at work as Thomas puffed along.

Later, Thomas saw the tractor close by.

"Hullo," said the tractor. "I'm Terence. I'm plowing."

"I'm Thomas. I'm pulling a train. What ugly wheels you've got."

"They're not ugly, they're caterpillars," said Terence. "I can go anywhere. I don't need rails."

"I don't want to go anywhere," said Thomas. "I like my rails, thank you."

Winter came with dark clouds full of snow.

"I don't like it," said Thomas' Driver. "A heavy fall is coming. I hope it doesn't stop us."

"Pooh!" said Thomas. "Soft stuff, nothing to it." And he puffed on, feeling cold but confident.

They finished their journey safely, but by now the country was covered.

"You'll need your snowplow for the next journey, Thomas," said his Driver.

"Pooh! Snow is silly, soft stuff—it won't stop me."

The snowplow was heavy and uncomfortable and made Thomas cross. He shook it and he banged it—and when they got back, it was so damaged that the Driver had to take it off.

"You're a very naughty engine," he said to Thomas.

Next morning, Thomas' Driver and Fireman came early and worked hard to mend the snowplow, but they couldn't make it fit.

Thomas was pleased. "I shan't have to wear it, I shan't have to wear it," he puffed to Annie and Clarabel.

But they were rather worried. "I hope it's all right, I hope it's all right," they whispered to each other.

The Driver was worried, too. "It's not bad here," he said to the Fireman, "but it's sure to be deep in the valley."

"Silly, soft stuff," puffed Thomas. "I didn't need that stupid old thing yesterday, and I shan't today. Snow can't stop me."

He rushed into a tunnel, thinking how clever he was. But there was trouble ahead.

"Cinders and ashes," said Thomas. "I'm stuck." And he was.

"Back, Thomas. Back," said his Driver.

Thomas tried, but his wheels spun and he couldn't move.

The Conductor went back for help while everyone else tried to dig the snow away. But as fast as they dug, more snow slipped down, until Thomas was nearly buried.

"Oh, my wheels and coupling rods. I shall have to stop here till I'm frozen. What a silly engine I am." And Thomas began to cry.

At last, a bus came to rescue the passengers.

And then who should come to Thomas' rescue but Terence. Snow never worries him.

He pulled the empty coaches away, then came back for Thomas.

Thomas' wheels were clear but still spun when he tried to move. Terence tugged and slipped and slipped and tugged, and at last dragged Thomas clear of the snow, ready for the journey home.

"Thank you, Terence. Your caterpillars are splendid," said Thomas.

"I hope you'll be sensible now, Thomas," said his Driver.

"I'll try," said Thomas, and he puffed slowly away.

Double Trouble

It was a beautiful morning on the Island of Sodor.

Thomas the Tank Engine's blue paint sparkled in the sunshine as he puffed happily along his Branch Line with Annie and Clarabel.

He was feeling very pleased with himself.

"Hullo, Thomas," whistled Percy. "You look splendid!"

"Yes, indeed," boasted Thomas. "Blue is the only proper color for an engine."

"Oh, I don't know. I like my brown paint," said Toby.

"I've always been green. I wouldn't want to be any other color, either," added Percy.

"Well, well, anyway," huffed Thomas, "blue is the only color for a—for a Really Useful Engine. Everyone knows that."

Percy said no more. He just grinned at Toby.

Later, Thomas was resting when Percy arrived. A large hopper was loading his freight cars full of coal.

Thomas was still being cheeky. “Careful,” he warned. “Watch out with those silly cars.”

“Go on. Go on,” muttered the cars.

“And by the way,” went on Thomas, “those buffers don’t look very safe to me—”

The last load poured down.

"Help, help!" cried Thomas. "Get me out!"

Percy was worried, but he couldn't help laughing. Thomas' smart blue paint was covered in coal dust from smokebox to bunker.

"Ha, ha!" chuckled Percy. "You don't look Really Useful now, Thomas. You look really disgraceful."

"I'm not disgraceful," choked Thomas. "You did that on purpose. Get me out!"

It took so long to clean Thomas that he wasn't in time for his next train. Toby had to take Annie and Clarabel.

"Poor Thomas," whispered Annie to Clarabel. They were most upset.

Thomas was grumpy in the Shed that night.

Toby thought it a great joke, but Percy was cross with Thomas for thinking he had made his paint dirty on purpose. "Fancy a Really Useful Blue Engine like Thomas becoming a disgrace to Sir Topham Hatt's railway."

Next day, Thomas was feeling more cheerful as he watched Percy bring his cars from the junction. The cars were heavy, and Percy was tired.

"Have a drink," said his Driver. "Then you'll feel better."

The water column stood at the end of the siding with the unsafe buffers.

Suddenly Percy found that he couldn't stop. The buffers didn't stop him, either. "Ooh," wailed Percy. "Help!" The buffers were broken, and Percy was wheel-deep in coal.

It was time for Thomas to leave. He had seen everything. "Now Percy has learned his lesson, too," he chuckled to himself.

That night, the two engines made up their quarrel.

"I didn't cause your accident on purpose, Thomas," whispered Percy. "You do know that, don't you?"

"Of course," replied Thomas. "And I'm sorry I teased you. Your green paint looks splendid again, too. In future, we'll both be more careful of coal."

Old Iron

One day, James had to wait at the station till Edward and his train came in. This made him cross. "Late again!"

Edward laughed, and James fumed away.

After James had finished his work, he went back to the Yard and puffed onto the turntable.

He was still feeling very bad-tempered. “Edward is impossible,” he grumbled to the others. “He clanks about like a lot of old iron, and he is so slow he makes us wait!”

Thomas and Percy were indignant. “Old iron! Slow? Why, Edward could beat you in a race any day!”

“Really!” said James. “I should like to see him do it!”

Next morning, James’ Driver was suddenly taken ill. He could hardly stand, so the Fireman uncoupled James ready for shunting.

James was impatient.

Suddenly the Signalman shouted. There was James puffing away down the line.

"All traffic halted," he announced at last. Then he told the Fireman what had happened.

"Two boys were on James' footplate fiddling with the controls."

"Phew!"

"They tumbled off and ran when James started."

Brriinngg!

The Signalman answered the telephone. "Yes . . . he's here. . . . Right. I'll tell him.

"The Inspector's coming at once. He wants a shunter's pole and a coil of wire rope."

"What for?" wondered the Fireman.

"Search me! But you'd better get them quickly."

The Fireman was ready when Edward arrived. The Inspector saw the pole and the rope. "Good man. Jump in."

"We'll catch him, we'll catch him," puffed Edward.

James was laughing.

"What a lark! What a lark!" He chuckled to himself.

Suddenly he was going faster and faster. He realized that he had no Driver! "What shall I do? I can't stop! Help! Help!"

"We're coming! We're coming!" called Edward.

Edward was panting up behind with every ounce of steam he had. At last, he caught up with James.

"Steady, Edward!" called his Driver.

The Inspector stood on Edward's front, holding a noose of rope in the crook of the shunter's pole. He was trying to slip it over James' buffer. The engines swayed and lurched.

At last! "Got him!" he shouted. He pulled the noose tight.

Gently braking, Edward's Driver checked the engine's speed, and James' Fireman scrambled across and took control.

"So the 'old iron' caught you after all," chuckled Edward.

"I'm sorry," whispered James. "Thank you for saving me. You were splendid, Edward."

"That's all right," replied Edward.
The engines arrived at the station side by side.

Sir Topham Hatt was waiting. "A fine piece of work," he said. "James, you can rest and then take your train. I'm proud of you, Edward. You shall go to the Works and have your worn parts mended."

"Oh, thank you, Sir," said Edward. "It'll be lovely not to clank."

Percy Takes the Plunge

One day, Henry wanted to rest, but Percy was talking to some engines. He was telling them about the time he had braved bad weather to help Thomas.

"It was raining hard. Water swirled under my boiler. I couldn't see where I was going, but I struggled on."

“Oooh, Percy, you are brave.”

“Well, it wasn’t anything, really. Water’s nothing to an engine with determination.”

“Tell us more, Percy.”

“What are you engines doing here?” hissed Henry. “This shed is for Sir Topham Hatt’s engines. Go away! Silly things!” Henry snorted.

“They’re not silly.” Percy had been enjoying himself.

“They are silly, and so are you. ‘Water’s nothing to an engine with determination.’ Huh!”

"Anyway," said cheeky Percy, "I'm not afraid of water. I like it." He ran off to the harbor singing:

"Once an engine attached to a train
Was afraid of a few drops of rain. . . ."

"No one ever lets me forget the time I wouldn't come out of the tunnel in case the rain spoiled my paint," huffed Henry.

Thomas was looking at a board on the quay. DANGER.

"We mustn't go past it," he said. "That's orders."

"Why?"

"'DANGER' means falling down something," said Thomas. "I went past 'DANGER' once and fell down a mine."

"I can't see a mine," said Percy. He didn't know that the foundations of the quay had sunk. The rails now sloped downward to the sea.

"Stupid board!" said Percy.

Percy made a plan.

One day, he whispered to the cars, "Will you give me a bump when we get to the quay?"

The cars had never been *asked* to bump an engine before. They giggled and chattered about it.

"Driver doesn't know my plan," chuckled Percy.

"On! On! On!" laughed the cars.

Percy thought they were helping. "I'll pretend to stop at the station, but the cars will push me past the board. Then I'll make them stop. I can do that whenever I like."

Every wise engine knows that you cannot trust freight cars.

"Go on! Go on!" they yelled, and bumped Percy's Driver and Fireman off the footplate.

"Ow!" said Percy, sliding past the board.

Percy was frantic. "That's enough!"

Percy was sunk.

"You are a very disobedient engine."

Percy knew that voice. "Please, Sir, get me out, Sir. I'm truly sorry, Sir."

"No, Percy, we cannot do that till high tide. I hope it will teach you to take care of yourself."

"Yes, Sir."

It was dark when they brought floating cranes to rescue Percy. He was too cold and stiff to move by himself.

Next day, he was sent to the Works on Henry's freight train.

"Well, well, well!" chuckled Henry. "Did you like the water?"

"No!"

"I am surprised. You need more determination, Percy. 'Water's nothing to an engine with determination,' you know. Perhaps you will like it better next time."

Percy is quite determined that there won't be a next time!

A Cow on the Line

Edward was getting old. His bearings were worn, and he clanked as he puffed along. He was taking empty cattle cars to a market town.

The sun shone, birds sang, but Edward was heading for trouble.

"Come on. Come on," he puffed.

"Oh! Oh! Oh! Oh!" screamed the cars.

Edward puffed and clanked. The cars rattled and screamed.

Some cows were grazing nearby. They were not used to trains. The noise and smoke disturbed them.

As Edward clanked by, they broke through the fence and ran across the line. A coupling was broken, and some cars were left behind.

Edward felt a jerk but didn't take much notice. He was used to cattle cars.

"Bother those cars," he thought. "Why can't they come quietly!" He was at the next station before either he or his Driver realized what had happened.

When Gordon and Henry heard about the accident, they laughed and boasted. "Fancy allowing cows to break his train. They wouldn't dare do that to us. We'd show them!"

Old Toby was cross. "You couldn't help it, Edward. They've never met cows. I have, and I know the trouble they are."

Some days later, Gordon rushed through Edward's station. "*Poop, poop!* Mind the cows! Hurry, hurry, hurry," puffed Gordon.

"Don't make such a fuss. Don't make such a fuss," grumbled his coaches.

A long stretch of line lay ahead. In the distance was a bridge. It seemed to Gordon that there was something on the bridge. His Driver thought so, too.

"Whoa, Gordon!" he said, and shut off steam.

"Pooh!" said Gordon. "It's only a cow! SHOO! SHOO!"

He moved slowly onto the bridge, but the cow wouldn't "shoo."

She had lost her calf and felt lonely. *"Moo!"* she said sadly. Everyone tried to send her away, but she wouldn't go.

Henry arrived. "What's this? A cow! I'll soon settle her. Be off! Be off!"

"Moo!" said the cow.

Henry backed away nervously. "I don't want to hurt her."

At the next station, Henry's Conductor told them about the cow and warned the Signalman that the line was blocked.

"That must be Bluebell," said the Porter. "Her calf is here, looking for her mother. Percy will take her along."

At the bridge, Bluebell was very pleased to see her calf again, and the Porter led them away.

"Not a word. Keep it dark," whispered Gordon and Henry to each other. They felt rather silly. But the story soon spread.

"Well, well, well," chuckled Edward. "Two big engines afraid of a cow."

"Afraid? Rubbish!" said Gordon. "We didn't want the poor thing to hurt herself by running up against us. We stopped so as not to excite her. You see what I mean, my dear Edward."

"Yes, Gordon," said Edward.

Gordon felt somehow that Edward saw only too well!

Bertie's Chase

"Stop, stop! I've got Thomas' passengers!" wailed Bertie, roaring up to the gates. It was no good. Edward was gone.

"Bother," said Bertie. "Bother Thomas' Fireman not coming to work today. Why did I promise to help the passengers catch the train?"

"That will do, Bertie," said his Driver. "A promise is a promise, and we must keep it."

"I'll catch Edward or bust," said Bertie.

"Oh, my gears and axles," he groaned, toiling up the hill. "I'll never be the same bus again.

"Hurray! Hurray! I see him," cheered Bertie as he reached the top.

"Oh, no! Edward's at the station. No . . . he's stopped at a crossing. Hurray! Hurray!"

Bertie tore down the hill.

"Well done, Bertie!" shouted his passengers. "Go it!"

Bertie skidded into the yard. "Wait! Wait!" cried Bertie. He was just in time to see Edward puff away. "I'm sorry," said Bertie.

"Never mind," said the passengers. "After him, quickly—third time lucky, you know. Do you think we'll catch him at the next station, Driver?"

"There's a good chance," replied the Driver. "Our road keeps close to the line, and we can climb hills better than Edward. I'll just make sure." He spoke to the Station Master. Bertie and the passengers waited impatiently.

"Yes, we'll do it this time," said the Driver.

"Hurray," called the passengers as Bertie chased after Edward once more.

"This hill is too steep! This hill is too steep!" grumbled the coaches as Edward snorted in front.

They reached the top at last and ran smoothly into the station.

"Peee-eep!" whistled Edward. "Get in quickly, please."

The Conductor blew the whistle, and Edward's Driver looked back. But the flag didn't wave. Then he heard Bertie.

Everything seemed to happen at once—and the Station Master told the Conductor and Driver what had happened.

"I'm sorry about the chase, Bertie," said Edward.

"My fault," replied Bertie. "Late at junction . . . you didn't know . . . about Thomas' passengers."

"*Peep peep!* Goodbye, Bertie, we're off," whistled Edward.

“Three cheers for Bertie!” called the passengers.

Bertie raced back to tell Thomas that all was well.

“Thank you, Bertie, for keeping your promise,” said Thomas. “You’re a very good friend indeed.”

James in a Mess

Toby and Henrietta were enjoying their new job on the Island of Sodor, but they do look old-fashioned and did need new paint.

James was very rude whenever he saw them. "Yecch! What dirty objects!" he would say.

At last, Toby lost patience. "James," he asked, "why are you red?"

"I am a splendid engine," answered James, "ready for anything. You never see my paint dirty."

"Oh!" said Toby innocently. "That's why you once needed bootlaces—to be ready, I suppose."

James went redder than ever and snorted off. It was such an insult to be reminded of the time a bootlace had been used to mend a hole in his coaches.

At the end of the line, James left his coaches and got ready for his next train. It was a "slow freight," stopping at every station to pick up and set down cars.

James hated slow freight trains. "Dirty cars from dirty sidings! Yecch!"

Starting with only a few, he picked up more and more cars at each station till he had a long train.

At first, the freight cars behaved well, but James bumped them so crossly that they were determined to get back at him.

Presently, they approached the top of Gordon's Hill. Heavy freight trains halt here to set their brakes. James had had an accident with cars before and should have remembered this.

"Wait, James, wait," said the Driver, but James wouldn't wait. He was too busy thinking what he would say to Toby when they next met.

The freight cars' chance had come.

"Hurrah! Hurrah!" they laughed, and banging their buffers, they pushed him down the hill.

"On! On!" yelled the cars.

"I've got to stop! I've got to stop!" groaned James.

Disaster lay ahead.

Something sticky splashed all over James. He had run into two tar wagons and was black from smokebox to cab. He was more dirty than hurt, but the tar wagons and some cars were all to pieces.

Toby and Percy were sent to help and came as quickly as they could.

"Look here, Percy!" exclaimed Toby. "Whatever is that dirty object?"

"That's James. Didn't you know?"

"It's James' shape," said Toby, "but James is a splendid red engine, and you never see his paint dirty."

James pretended he hadn't heard.

Toby and Percy cleared away the unhurt cars and helped James home.

Sir Topham Hatt met them.

"Well done, Percy and Toby." He turned to James. "Fancy letting your cars run away. I *am* surprised. You're not fit to be seen; you must be cleaned at once. Toby shall have a new coat of paint."

"Please, Sir, can Henrietta have one, too?" said Toby.
"Certainly, Toby."
"Oh, thank you, Sir! She will be pleased."
All James could do was watch Toby as he ran off happily with the news.

Percy and the Signal

Percy works in the yard at the Big Station. He loves playing jokes, but they can get him into trouble.

One morning, he was very cheeky indeed. "*Peep peep!* Hurry up, Gordon! The train's ready."

Gordon thought he was late.

"Ha ha ha!" laughed Percy, and showed him a train of dirty coal trucks.

Gordon thought how to get back at Percy for teasing him.

Next it was James' turn.

"Stay in the Shed today, James. Sir Topham Hatt will come and see you."

"Ah!" thought James. "Sir Topham Hatt knows I'm a fine engine. He wants me to pull a Special Train."

James' Driver and Fireman could not make him move. The other engines grumbled dreadfully. They had to do James' work as well as their own.

At last, the Inspector arrived. "Show a wheel, James. You can't stay here all day."

"Sir Topham Hatt told me to stay here. He sent a message this morning."

"He did not. How could he? He's away for a week."

"Oh!" said James. "Oh! Where's Percy?" Percy had wisely disappeared!

When Sir Topham Hatt came back, he was cross with James and Percy for causing so much trouble.

But the very next day, Percy was still being cheeky. “I say, you engines, I’m to take some freight cars to Thomas’ Junction. Sir Topham Hatt chose me especially. He must know I’m a Really Useful Engine.”

“More likely he wants you out of the way,” grunted James.

Gordon looked across to James. They were going to play a trick on Percy.

"James and I were just speaking about signals at the Junction. We can't be too careful about signals. But then I needn't say that to a Really Useful Engine like you, Percy."

Percy felt flattered.

"We had spoken of 'backing signals,' " put in James. "They need extra-special care, you know. Would you like me to explain?"

"No thank you, James," said Percy. "I know all about signals."

Percy was a little worried. "I wonder what 'backing signals' are," he thought. "Never mind, I'll manage." He puffed crossly to his freight cars and felt better.

He came to a signal. “Bother! It’s at ‘danger.’ ”

The signal moved to show “line clear.” Its arm moved up instead of down. Percy had never seen that sort of signal before.

“Down means ‘go’ and up means ‘stop,’ so upper still must mean ‘go back.’ I know! It’s one of those ‘backing signals’ that Gordon told me about.”

"Come on, Percy," said his Driver. "Off we go. STOP! You're going the wrong way!"

"But it's a backing signal," Percy protested, and told him about Gordon and James. The Driver laughed and explained.

"Oh, dear!" said Percy. "Let's start quickly before they see us."

He was too late. Gordon saw everything.

That night, the big engines talked about signals. They thought the subject was funny! Percy thought they were being very silly!

Percy Proves a Point

Percy worked hard at the new harbor. The workmen needed stone for their building. Toby helped, but sometimes the loads of stone were too heavy, and Percy had to fetch them for himself. Sometimes he'd see Thomas.

"Well done, Percy. Sir Topham Hatt is very pleased with us."

An airfield was close by. Percy heard the airplanes zooming overhead all day. The noisiest of all was a helicopter.

"Silly thing!" said Percy. "Why can't it go and buzz somewhere else?"

One day, Percy stopped at the airfield. "Hullo!" said Percy. "Who are you?"

"I'm Harold. Who are you?"

"I'm Percy. What whirly great arms you've got."

"They're nice arms," said Harold. "I can hover like a bird. Don't you wish *you* could hover?"

"Certainly not—I like my rails, thank you."

"I think railways are slow," said Harold. "They're not much use and quite out-of-date." He whirled his arms and buzzed away.

Percy found Toby at the Quarry. "I say, Toby—that Harold, that stuck-up whirlybird thing, says I'm slow and out-of-date. Just let him wait. I'll show him!"

He collected his freight cars and started off, still fuming.

Soon they heard a familiar buzzing.

"Percy," whispered his Driver, "there's Harold. He's not far ahead. Let's race him."

"Yes, let's!" said Percy.

Percy pounded along. The cars screamed and swayed.

"Well, I'll be a ding-dong-danged!" said the Driver. There was Harold—the race was on!

"Go it, Percy!" he yelled. "You're gaining!"

Percy had never been allowed to run fast before. He was having the time of his life.

"Hurry! Hurry! Hurry!" he panted to the cars.

"We don't want to, we don't want to," they grumbled. It was no use. Percy was bucketing along with flying wheels, and Harold was high and alongside.

The Fireman shoveled for dear life.

"Well done, Percy," shouted the Driver. "We're gaining! We're going ahead! Oh, good boy, good boy!"

A "distant signal" warned them that the harbor wharf was near. *"Peep, peep, peep!"*

"Brakes, Conductor, please." The Driver carefully checked the train's headlong speed.

They rolled under the Main Line and halted on the wharf.

"Oh, dear!" groaned Percy. "I'm sure we've lost."

The Fireman scrambled to the cab roof. "We've won! We've won!" he shouted. "Harold's still hovering. He's looking for a place to land!"

"Listen, boys!" the Fireman called. "Here's a song for Percy:

Said Harold the Helicopter to our Percy, 'You are slow!
Your Railway is out-of-date and not much use, you know.'
But Percy with his stone cars did the trip in record time,
And we beat the helicopter on our old Branch Line."

Percy loved it. "Oh, thank you!" he said. He liked the last line best of all and was a very happy engine.

Pop Goes the Diesel

Duck is very proud of being Great Western. He talks endlessly about it. But he works hard, too, and makes everything go like clockwork.

It was a splendid day.

The cars and coaches behaved well. The passengers even stopped grumbling!

But the engines didn't like having to bustle about. "There are two ways of doing things," Duck told them. "The Great Western way, or the wrong way. I'm Great Western and—"

"Don't we know it," they groaned.

The engines were glad when a visitor came. He purred smoothly towards them.

Sir Topham Hatt introduced him. "Here is Diesel. I have agreed to give him a trial. He needs to learn. Please teach him, Duck."

"Good morning," purred Diesel in an oily voice. "Pleased to meet you, Duck. Is that James—and Henry—and Gordon, too? I am delighted to meet such famous engines."

The silly engines were flattered. "He has very good manners," they murmured. "We are pleased to have him in our Yard."

Duck had his doubts. "Come on," he said.
Diesel purred after him.
"Your worthy Top—"
"Sir Topham Hatt to you," ordered Duck.

Diesel looked hurt. "Your worthy Sir Topham Hatt thinks I need to learn. He is mistaken. We diesels don't need to learn. We know everything. We come to a Yard and improve it. We are revolutionary."

"Oh!" said Duck. "If you're revo-thingummy, perhaps you would collect my cars while I fetch Gordon's coaches."

Diesel, delighted to show off, purred away.

When Duck returned, Diesel was trying to take some cars from a siding. They were old and empty. They had not been touched for a long time. Diesel found them hard to move.

Pull—push—backwards—forwards! *"Oh-eeeer! Oh-eeeer!"* the cars groaned. "We can't! We won't!"

Duck watched with interest.

Diesel lost patience.

"GrrRRRrrrRRR!" he roared, and gave a great heave. The cars jerked forward.

"Oh-eeeer! Oh-eeeer!" they screamed. "We can't! We *won't!*" Some of their brakes snapped, and the gear jammed in the sleepers.

"GrrrrRRRRrrrrRRRRrrrrRRRR!"

"Ho! Ho! Ho!" chuckled Duck.

Diesel recovered and tried to push the cars back, but they wouldn't move. Duck ran quietly round to collect the other cars. "Thank you for arranging these, Diesel. I must go now."

"Don't you want this lot?"

"No, thank you."

Diesel gulped. "And I've taken all this trouble. Why didn't you tell me?"

"You never asked me. Besides," said Duck, "you were having such fun being rev-whatever-it-was-you-said. Goodbye."

"GrrrRRRrrrRRR!" Diesel had to help the workmen clear the mess. He hated it. All the cars were laughing and singing at him.

"Cars are waiting in the Yard; tackling them with ease'll
'Show the world what I can do,' gaily boasts the Diesel.
In and out he creeps about, like a big black weasel.
When he pulls the wrong cars out—pop goes the Diesel!"

"Grrr!" growled Diesel, and scuttled away to sulk in the Shed.

Diesel's Devious Deed

Diesel, the new engine, was sulking. The freight cars would not stop singing rudely at him. Duck was horrified. "Shut up!" he ordered, and bumped them hard. "I'm sorry our cars were rude to you, Diesel."

Diesel was still furious. "It's all your fault. You made them laugh at me."

"Nonsense," said Henry. "Duck would never do that. We engines have our differences, but we never talk about them to the cars. That would be dis . . . dis . . ."

"Disgraceful!" said Gordon.

"Disgusting!" put in James.

"Despicable!" finished Henry.

Diesel hated Duck. He wanted him to be sent away, so he made a plan. He was going to tell lies about Duck.

Next day, he spoke to the cars. "I see you like jokes. You made a good joke about me yesterday. I laughed and laughed. Duck told me one about Gordon. I'll whisper it. . . . Don't tell Gordon I told you." And he sniggered away.

"Haw! Haw! Haw!" guffawed the cars. "Gordon will be cross with Duck when he knows. Let's tell him and get back at Duck for bumping us."

They laughed rudely at the engines as they went by.

Soon Gordon, Henry, and James found out why.

"Disgraceful!" said Gordon.

"Disgusting!" said James.

"Despicable!" said Henry. "We cannot allow it."

They consulted together. "Yes," they said, "he did it to us. We'll do it to him, and see how he likes it."

Duck was tired out. The cars had been cheeky and troublesome. He wanted to rest in the Shed.

The three engines barred his way. "*Hoooooooosh!* Keep out!"

"Stop fooling," said Duck. "I'm tired."

"So are we," hissed the engines. "We are tired of you. We like Diesel. We don't like you. You tell tales about us to the cars."

"I don't."

"You do."

"I don't."

"You do."

Sir Topham Hatt came to stop the noise.

"Duck called me a 'galloping sausage,' " spluttered Gordon.

". . . 'rusty red scrap iron,' " hissed James.

". . . I'm 'old square wheels,' " fumed Henry.

"Well, Duck?"

Duck considered. "I only wish, Sir," he said gravely, "that I'd thought of those names myself. If the dome fits . . ."

"He made cars laugh at us," accused the engines.

Sir Topham Hatt recovered. He'd been trying not to laugh himself. "Did you, Duck?"

"Certainly not, Sir. No steam engine would be as mean as that."

Diesel lurked up.

"Now, Diesel, you heard what Duck said."

"I can't understand it, Sir. To think that Duck, of all engines . . . I'm dreadfully grieved, Sir, but know nothing."

"I see," said Sir Topham Hatt. Diesel squirmed and hoped he didn't.

"I'm sorry, Duck, but you must go to Edward's station for a while. I know he will be glad to see you."

"As you wish, Sir."

Duck trundled sadly away while Diesel smirked with triumph.

A Close Shave for Duck

Duck the Great Western Engine puffed sadly to Edward's station. "It's not fair," he complained. "Diesel has been telling lies about me and made Sir Topham Hatt and all the engines think I'm horrid."

Edward smiled. "I know you aren't, and so does Sir Topham Hatt. You wait and see. Why don't you help me with these cars?"

Duck felt happier with Edward and set to work at once.

The cars were silly, heavy, and noisy. The two engines had to work hard, pushing and pulling all afternoon.

At last they reached the top of the hill.

"Goodbye," whistled Duck, and rolled gently over the crossing to the other line.

Duck loved coasting down the hill, running easily with the wind whistling past.

Suddenly—*Tweeeet!*

It was a conductor's warning whistle.

"Hurrah! Hurrah! Hurrah!" laughed the cars. "We've broken away. We've broken away. Chase him, bump him, throw him off the rails," they yelled.

"Hurry, Duck, hurry!" said the Driver.

They raced through Edward's station, but the cars were catching up. "As fast as we can—then they'll catch us gradually." The Driver was gaining control. "Another clear mile and we'll do it. Oh, glory! Look at that!"

James was just pulling out on their line from the station ahead. Any minute, there could be a crash.

"It's up to you now, Duck," cried the Driver.

Duck put every ounce of weight and steam against the cars.

"It's too late!" Duck groaned, and shut his eyes. He veered into a siding where a barber had set up shop. He was shaving a customer.

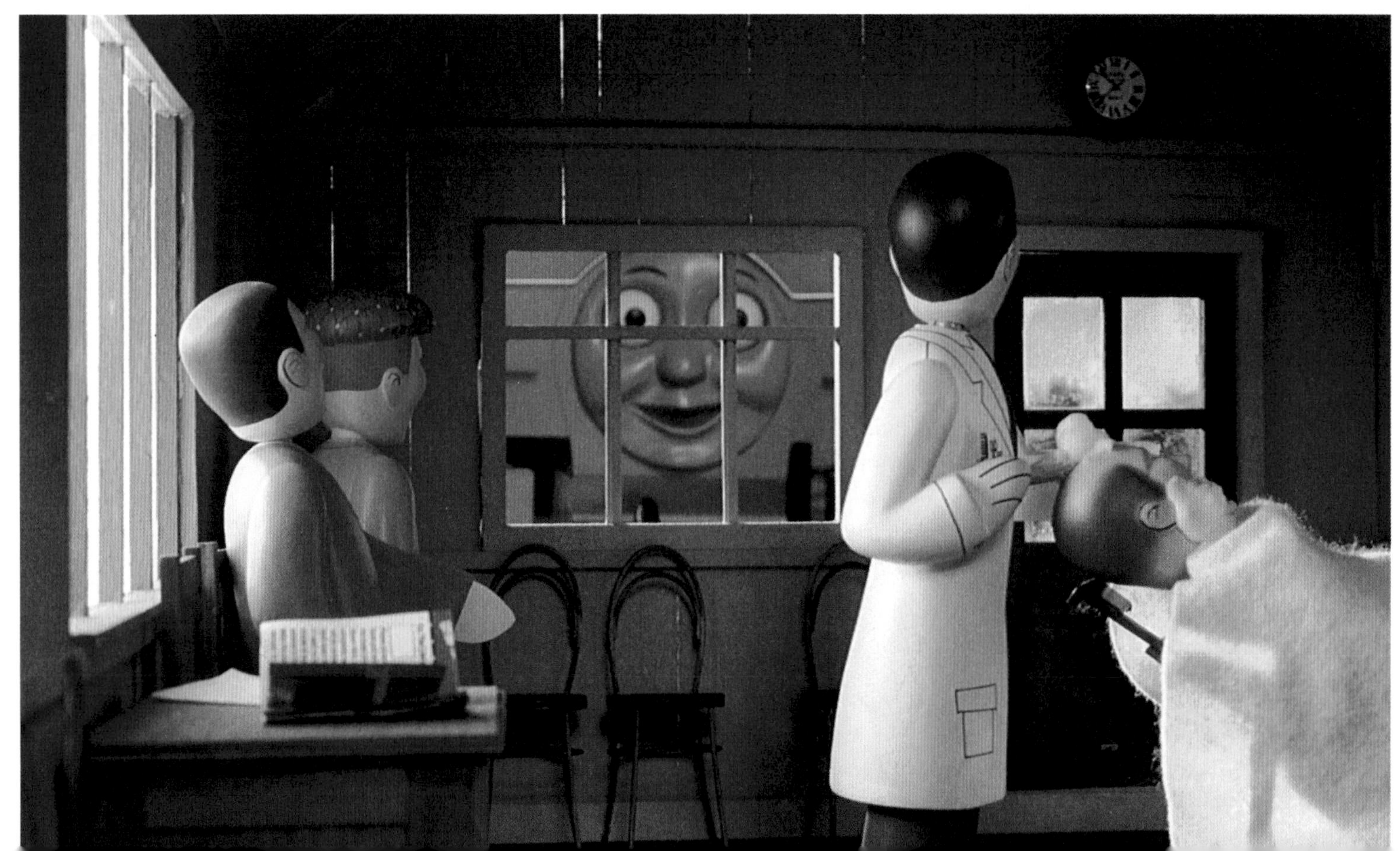

The silly cars had knocked their Conductor off his van and left him far behind after he had whistled a warning. But the cars didn't care. They were feeling very pleased with themselves.

"Beg pardon, sir!" gasped Duck. "Excuse my intrusion."

"No, I won't!" said the barber. "You've frightened my customers. I'll teach you." And he lathered Duck's face all over.

Poor Duck!

Thomas was helping to pull the cars away when Sir Topham Hatt arrived.

"I do not like engines popping through my walls," fumed the barber.

"I appreciate your feelings," said Sir Topham Hatt, "but you must know that this engine and his crew have prevented a serious accident. It was a very close—um—shave!"

"Oh!" said the barber. "Oh, excuse me." He filled a basin of water to wash Duck's face. "I'm sorry. I didn't know you were being a brave engine."

"That's all right, sir. I didn't know that either."

"You were very brave indeed," said Sir Topham Hatt. "I'm proud of you."

Sir Topham Hatt watched the rescue operation. Then he had more news for Duck. "And when you are properly washed and mended, you are coming home."

"Home, Sir? Do you mean the Yard?"

"Of course."

"But, Sir, they don't like me. They like Diesel."

"Not now. I never believed Diesel, so I sent him packing. The engines are sorry and want you back."

A few days later when he came home, there was a really rousing welcome for Duck the Great Western Engine.

Woolly Bear

In the summer, the work crews cut the long grass along the tracks—raking it into heaps to dry in the sun.

At this time of year, Percy stops where they have been cutting. The men load up his empty wagons, and he pulls them to the station.

Toby then takes them to the hills for the farmers to feed their stock.

"Wheeeeeeeesh!" Percy gave a ghostly whistle. "Don't be frightened, Thomas." He laughed. "It's only me!"

"Your ugly fizz is enough to frighten anyone," said Thomas. "You're like—"

"Ugly indeed! I'm—"

"—a green caterpillar with red stripes," continued Thomas firmly. "You crawl like one, too."

"I don't!"

"Who's been late every afternoon this week?"

"It's the hay."

"I can't help that," said Thomas. "Time's time, and Sir Topham Hatt relies on me to keep it. I can't if you crawl in the hay till all hours."

“ ‘Green caterpillar’ indeed!” fumed Percy as he set off to collect some hay to take to the harbor. “Everyone says I’m handsome—or at least nearly everyone. Anyway, my curves are better than Thomas’ corners. Thomas says I’m always late,” he grumbled. “I’m never late—or at least only a few minutes. What’s that to Thomas? He can always catch up time farther on.”

All the same, he and his Driver decided to start home early. Then came trouble.

A crate of treacle was upset all over Percy.
Percy was cross. He was still sticky when he puffed away.

The wind was blowing fiercely.

"Look at that!" exclaimed the Driver.

The wind caught the piled hay, tossing it up and over the track.

The line climbed here. "Take a run at it, Percy," his Driver advised.

Percy gathered speed. But the hay made the rails slippery, and his wheels wouldn't grip. Time after time, he stalled with spinning wheels and had to wait until the line ahead was cleared before he could start again.

Everyone was waiting. Thomas seethed impatiently. "Ten minutes late! I warned him. Passengers'll complain, and Sir Topham Hatt . . ."

Then they all saw Percy. They laughed and shouted. "Sorry I'm late!" Percy panted.

"Look what's crawled out of the hay!" teased Thomas.

"What's wrong?" asked Percy.

"Talk about hairy caterpillars!" puffed Thomas. "It's worth being late to have seen you."

When Percy got home, his Driver showed him what he looked like in a mirror.

"Bust my buffers! No wonder they all laughed. I'm just like a woolly bear! Please clean me before Toby comes." But it was no good. Thomas told Toby all about it.

Instead of talking about sensible things like playing ghosts, Thomas and Toby made jokes about "woolly bear" caterpillars and other creatures which crawl about in hay.

They laughed a lot, but Percy thought they were really being very silly indeed.

Donald and Douglas

Donald and Douglas are twins and had arrived from Scotland to help Sir Topham Hatt—but only one engine had been expected.

The twins meant well, but did cause confusion. Sir Topham Hatt had given them numbers—Donald 9 and Douglas 10—but he was still planning to send one engine home.

There was a brake van in the Yard that had taken a dislike to Douglas. Things always went wrong when he had to take it out. His trains were late, and he was blamed. Douglas began to worry.

Donald, his twin, was angry. "You're a muckle nuisance," said Donald. "It's to leave ye behind I'd be wantin'."

"You can't," said the brake van. "I'm essential."

"Och, are ye?" Donald burst out. "You're nothin' but a screechin' and a noise when all is said and done. Spite Dougie, would ye? Take that!"

"Oh! Ooh!" cried the van.

"There's more coming should you misbehave."

The van behaved better after that.

Until one day Donald had an accident. The rails were slippery. He couldn't stop in time.

Donald wasn't hurt, but Sir Topham Hatt was most annoyed. "I am disappointed, Donald. I didn't expect such—um—clumsiness from you. I had decided to send Douglas back and keep you."

"I'm sorry, Sir," said Donald.

"I should think so, too. You have upset my arrangements. Now James will have to help with the goods work while you have your tender mended. James won't like that."

Sir Topham Hatt was right. James grumbled dreadfully about his extra work.

"Anyone would think," said Douglas, "that Donald had had his accident on purpose. I heard tell about an engine and some tar wagons."

"Shut up!" said James. "It's not funny." He didn't like to be reminded of his own accident.

"Well, well, well. Surely, James, it wasn't you? You didn't say!"

James didn't say. He slouched sulkily away.

"James is cross," snickered the spiteful brake van. "We'll try to make him crosser still!"

"Hold back!" giggled the freight cars to each other.

James did his best, but he was exhausted when they reached Edward's station. Luckily, Douglas was there.

"Help me up the hill, please," panted James. "These freight cars are playing tricks."

"We'll show them," said Douglas.

Slowly but surely, the snorting engines forced the freight cars up the hill.

But James was losing steam. "I can't do it. I can't do it!"

"Leave it to me!" shouted Douglas.

The Conductor was anxious. "Go steady! The van's breaking."

The van was in pieces.

No one had been hurt, but soon Edward came to clear the mess. Sir Topham Hatt was on board. "I might have known it would be Douglas!" he said.

"Douglas was grand, Sir," said Edward. "James had no steam left, but Douglas worked hard enough for three. I heard him from my yard."

"Two would have been enough," said Sir Topham Hatt. "I want to be fair, Douglas, but I don't know. I really don't know."

Sir Topham Hatt was making up his mind about which engine to send away—but that's another story.

9

The Deputation

Snow came early to the Island of Sodor. It was heavier than usual. Most engines hate snow. Donald and Douglas were used to it. Coupled back to back with a van between their tenders and a snowplow on their fronts, they set to work.

They puffed backwards and forwards, patrolling the line. Generally, the snow slipped away easily, but sometimes they found deeper drifts.

Presently, they came to a drift which was larger than most. They charged it, and were just backing for another try when . . .

"Help! Help!"

"Losh sakes, Donald, it's Henry! Don't worry yourself, Henry. Wait awhile. We'll have ye out!"

Henry was very grateful. He saw all was not well.

The twins were looking glum. They told him Sir Topham Hatt was making a decision. "He'll send us away for sure."

“It’s a shame!” said Percy.

“A lot of nonsense about a broken signal box,” grumbled Gordon.

“That spiteful brake van, too,” put in James. “Good riddance. That’s what I say.”

“The twins were splendid in the snow,” added Henry. “It isn’t fair.” They all agreed that something must be done, but none knew what.

Percy decided to talk to Edward about it. “What you need,” said Edward, “is a deputation.” He explained what that was.

Percy ran back quickly. “Edward says we need a depot-station.”

“Of course,” said Gordon, “the question is . . .”

“. . . what is a desperation?” asked Henry.

“It’s when engines tell Sir Topham Hatt something’s wrong,” said Percy.

“Did you say ‘tell Sir Topham Hatt’?” asked Duck thoughtfully. There was a long silence.

“I propose,” said Gordon, “that Percy be our—er—hum—disputation.”

"Me?" squeaked Percy. "I can't."

"Rubbish, Percy," said Henry. "It's easy."

"That's settled, then," said Gordon.

Poor Percy wished it wasn't.

"Hullo, Percy! It's nice to be back."

Percy jumped. "Er, y-y-yes, Sir, please, Sir."

"You look nervous, Percy. What's the matter?"

"Please, Sir, they've made me a desperation, Sir. To speak to you, Sir. I don't like it, Sir."

Sir Topham Hatt pondered. "Do you mean a deputation, Percy?"

"Yes, Sir, please, Sir. It's Donald and Douglas. They say, Sir, that if you send them away, Sir, well, they'll be turned into scrap, Sir. That would be dreadful, Sir. Please, Sir, don't send them away."

"Thank you, Percy. That will do."

Later, Sir Topham Hatt spoke to the engines. "I had a deputation. I understand your feelings, and I've given a lot of thought to the matter."

He paused impressively. "Donald and Douglas, I hear that your work in the snow was good. You shall have a new coat of paint."

The twins were surprised. "Thank ye, Sir."

"But your names will be painted on you. We'll have no more 'mistakes.' "

"Thank ye, Sir. Does this mean that the both of us . . . ?"
Sir Topham Hatt smiled. "It means—"
But the rest of his speech was drowned in a delighted chorus of cheers and whistles. The twins were here to stay.

BRENDAM BAY
BRENDAM BAY

The Diseasel

Bill and Ben are tank engine twins. Each has four wheels, a tiny chimney and dome, and a small, squat cab. Their freight cars are filled with china clay. It is needed for pottery, paper, paint, and many other things.

The twins are now kept busy pulling the cars for engines on the Main Line—and for ships in the harbor.

One morning, they arranged some cars and went away for more.

They returned to find them all gone. The twins were most surprised.

Their Drivers examined a patch of oil. "That's diesel," they said.

"It's a what'll?" asked Bill.

"A diseasel, I think," replied Ben. "There's a notice about them in our Shed."

"'Coughs and sneezles spread diseasels.' You had a cough in your smokebox yesterday. It's your fault the diseasel came."

"It isn't."

"It is."

"Stop arguing, you two," laughed their Drivers. "Let's go and rescue our freight cars."

Bill and Ben were horrified. "But the diseasel will magic us away, like the freight cars."

"He won't magic us," replied their Drivers. "We'll more likely magic him. Listen—he doesn't know you're twins. So we'll take away your names and numbers, and then this is what we'll do. . . ."

Puffing hard, the twins set off on their journey to find the diesel. They were looking forward to playing tricks on him.

Creeping into the Yard, they found the diesel on a siding with the missing cars. Ben hid behind, but Bill went boldly alongside.

The diesel looked up. "Do you *mind*?"

"Yes," said Bill. "I do. I want my cars back."

"These are mine," said the diesel. "Go away."

Bill pretended to be frightened. "You're a big bully," he whimpered. "You'll be sorry." He ran back and hid behind the cars on the other side.

Ben now came forward.

"Car stealer!" hissed Ben.

He ran away, too.

Bill took his place.

This went on and on till the diesel's eyes nearly popped out.

"Stop! You're making me giddy."

The two engines gazed at him.

"Are there two of you?"

"Yes, we're twins."

"I might have known it."

Just then, Edward bustled up. "Bill and Ben, why are you playing here?"

"We're not playing," protested Bill.

"We're rescuing our cars," squeaked Ben. "Even you don't take our cars without asking, but this diseasel did."

"There's no cause to be rude," said Edward severely. "This engine is a Metropolitan Vickers Diesel-Electric, Type 2."

The twins were most impressed. "We're sorry, Mr.—er . . ."

"Never mind." The diesel smiled. "Call me Boco. I'm sorry I didn't understand about the cars."

"That's all right, then," said Edward. "Now off you go, Bill and Ben. Fetch Boco's cars—then you take this lot.

"There's no real harm in them," he said to Boco, "but they're maddening at times."

Boco chuckled. " 'Maddening,' " he said, "is the word."

Edward's Exploit

Bertie the Bus was giving some visitors a tour of the Island of Sodor.

It was their last afternoon, and Edward was preparing to take them to meet Bill and Ben.

He found it hard to start the heavy train.

"Did you see him straining?" asked Henry.

"Positively painful," remarked James.

"Just pathetic," grunted Gordon. "He should give up and be preserved before it's too late."

"Shut up!" burst out Duck. "You're all jealous. Edward's better than any of you."

"You're right, Duck," said Boco. "Edward's old, but he'll surprise us all."

"I've done it! We're off! I've done it! We're off!" said Edward as he finally puffed out of the station.

Bill and Ben were delighted to see the visitors. They loved being photographed.

Later, they took the party to the China Clay Works in a "Brake Van Special."

Everyone had a splendid time, and the visitors were most impressed.

Then Edward took the visitors home.

On the way, the weather changed. Wind and rain buffeted Edward. His sanding gear failed, and his Fireman rode in front dropping sand on the rails by hand.

Suddenly Edward's wheels slipped fiercely, and with a shrieking crack, something broke.

The crew inspected the damage. Repairs took some time.

"One of your crankpins broke, Edward," said his Driver.

"We've taken your side rods off. Now you're like an old-fashioned engine. Can you get these people home? They must start back tonight."

"I'll try, sir," promised Edward.

Edward puffed and pulled his hardest, but his wheels kept slipping and he could not start the heavy train. The passengers were anxious.

The Driver, Fireman, and Conductor went along the train making adjustments between the coaches.

"We've loosened the couplings, Edward. Now you can pick your coaches up one by one, just as you do with freight cars."

"That'll be much easier," said Edward. "Come . . . on!" he puffed, and moved cautiously forward. The first coach moving helped to start the second, and the second helped the third.

"I've done it! I've done it!" puffed Edward.

"Steady, boy!" warned his Driver. "Well done, boy! You've got them! You've got them!" And he listened happily to Edward's steady beat as he forged slowly but surely ahead.

At last, battered, weary, but unbeaten, Edward steamed in.

Henry was waiting for the visitors with the Special Train.

"Peep! Peep!"

Sir Topham Hatt angrily pointed to the clock, but excited passengers cheered and thanked Edward, his Driver, and Fireman.

Duck and Boco saw to it that Edward was left in peace. Gordon and James remained respectfully silent.